This Book Belongs To:

_____

_____

# Meerkat

# Platypus

# Llama

# Alpaca

# Wombat

# Hedgehog

# Raccoon

# Porcupine

# Lemur

# Red Panda

# Sloth

# Fennec Fox

# Chameleon

# Axolotl

# Aardvark

# Armadillo

# Pangolin

# Dodo

# Tapir

# Komodo Dragon

# Quokka

# Pufferfish

# Kiwi Bird

# Skunk

# Sugar Glider

# Capybara

# Sea Otter

# Beaver

# PygmyGoat

# Blobfish

# Cockatoo

# Macaw

# Emu

# Ostrich

# Tamarin Monkey

# Marmoset

# Anglerfish

# Pufferfish

# Gecko

# Iguana

# Tarsier

# Flying Squirrel

# Star-Nosed Mole

# Dugong

# Spectacled Bear

# Octopus

# Galapagos Tortoise

# Narwhal

# Fairy Penguin

# BushBaby

# Frilled Lizard

We'd love to hear your feedback!
Simply scan the QR code below to share your thoughts

SCAN ME

Made in the USA
Monee, IL
29 December 2024